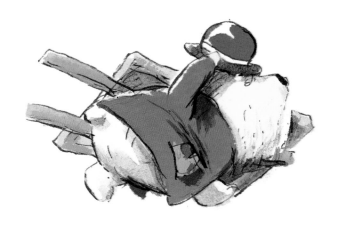

Goodness Gracious!

Goodness Gracious!

by Phil Cummings

illustrated by Craig Smith

ORCHARD BOOKS   New York

Goodness gracious! Look at my faces!

scary

starey

BOLD

or hairy

If you dare, look at my hair—

red *blue* SPIKY *too*

Jeepers creepers, look at my peepers!

weepy

sleepy

bright  or creepy

North and south, look at my mouth!

crabby

pouty

dribbly

SHOUTY

Chicken farms, look at my arms!

bendy   *bravey*

stretchy

wavy

Bristles, brussels, look at my muscles!

bulgy

bumpy

HUGE

or lumpy

Jumping jingers, look at my fingers!

clenched

or tricky

Pins, pegs, look at these legs!

short

long

bristly

strong

If you please, look at my knees—

crawly

knobbly

DIRTY

wobbly

Oh, Pirate Pete, look at my feet!

muddy

prickly

sloppy

sticky

Holy Moses! Look at my toeses!

chubby

grippy

careful

slippy

I'll open wide! Take a look inside—

teeth

tongue

tonsils

LUNGS

Now finallyyyyyyyyy,

look at meeeeeeeeeeeeeeee!

TA-DAH!

Good-bye.

Text copyright © 1989 by Phil Cummings
Illustrations copyright © 1989 by Craig Smith
First American Edition 1992 published by Orchard Books
First published in Australia by Omnibus Books

Orchard Books
387 Park Avenue South
New York, NY 10016

Manufactured in the United States of America
Printed by General Offset Company, Inc.
Bound by Horowitz / Rae
Book design by Susan Phillips

10 9 8 7 6 5 4 3 2 1

The text of this book is set in 32 point Bookman.

Library of Congress Cataloging-in-Publication Data
Cummings, Phil.
Goodness gracious! / by Phil Cummings ; illustrated by Craig Smith. — 1st American ed.
p.   cm.
Summary: A child celebrates the parts of her body while visualizing adventures
with pirates, dogs, baboons, and witches.
ISBN 0-531-05967-7. — ISBN 0-531-08567-8 (lib. bdg.)
[1. Body, Human—Fiction.   2. Stories in rhyme.]   I. Smith,
Craig, date,   ill.   II. Title.
PZ8.3.C8984Go   1991   [E]—dc20   91-17473